THE CLAM DIGGER'S BALL

Happy Reading!
♡ Robin

by Robin Taylor-Chiarello

Illustrated by Lisa Bohart

the Peppertree Press
www.peppertreepublishing.com

For information regarding permission,
call 941-922-2662 or contact us at our website:
www.peppertreepublishing.com or write to:
the Peppertree Press, LLC.
Attention: Publisher
1269 First Street, Suite 7
Sarasota, Florida 34236

ISBN: 978-1-61493-013-6

Library of Congress Number: 2011934773

Printed in the U.S.A.

Printed August 2011

"Amidst all the confusion and strife,
don't forget to celebrate life!"

I am Senator Sam Clam.
I live underground,
I make my home in Sandytown.

Welcome to SANDYTOWN

5

The story I'll tell you,
and I am very sincere...,
just took place
at our local town pier.

I was catching a nap
at my lovely mud flat,
when the beach started shaking
and I heard a big splat.

7

The sound of a shoe...
it's a rumble I knew.
It might be a clam digger!
What will I do?

Close up my clam shell.
Pull the alarm!
Warn all of my friends
they may be in harm!

Rake, rake, rake.
Shovel, shovel, shovel...
I know that sound,
and it sure means trouble!

12

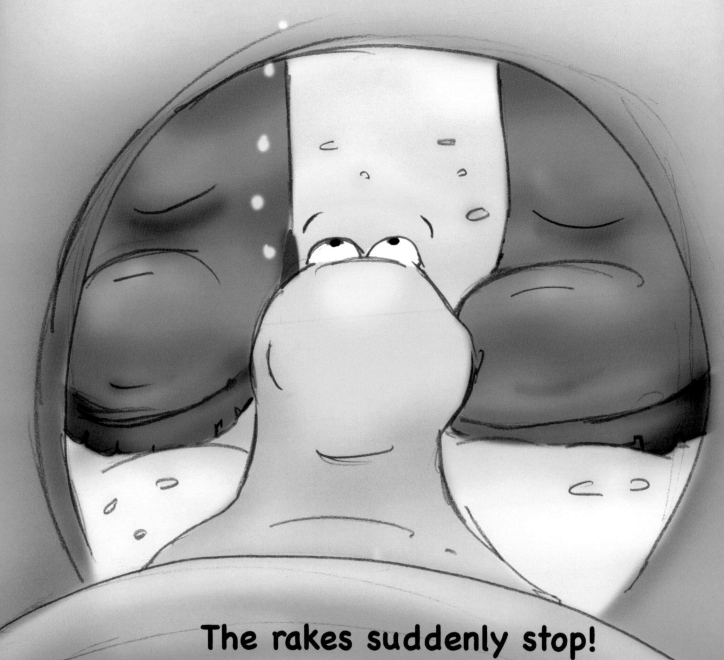

The rakes suddenly stop!
Daylight appears.
There is nowhere to go!
The humans are here!

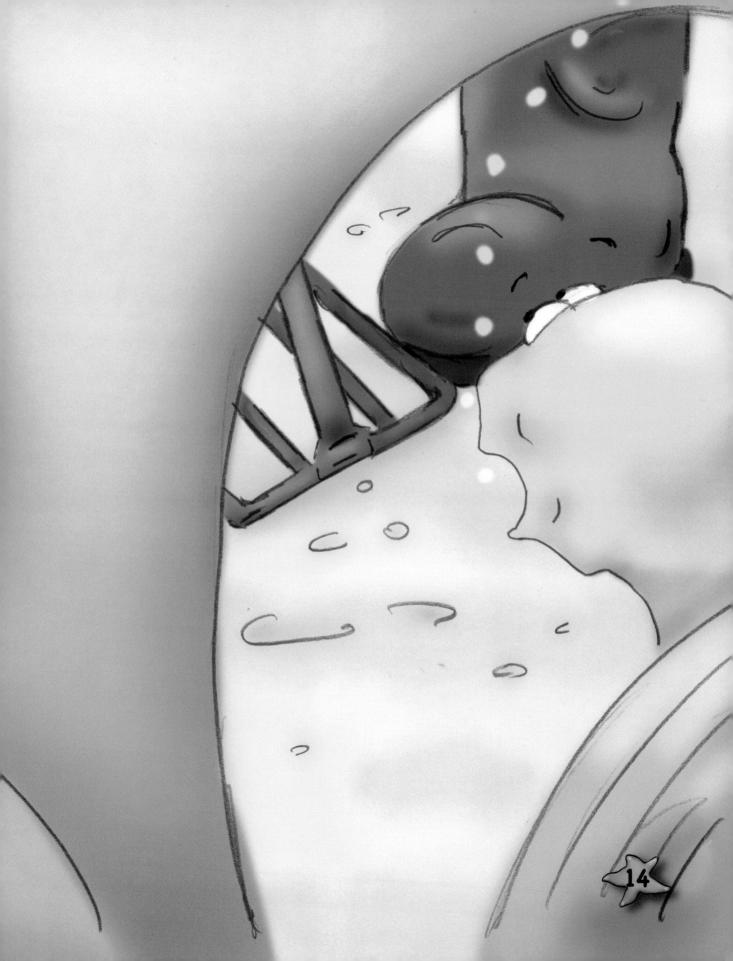

A big burly clam digger
shouts with disgust:
"We don't want these clams!
They are too big for us!"

Ladies in ruffles,
feathers and bows.
Don't forget shoes,
or just paint your toes!

19

Henry and Irving,
Marty and Max,
put on your tuxedos,
and grab your top hats!

20

Invite the mollusks
and sea life we know:
the parrot fish twins
that have nowhere to go!

23

The snails love to dance,
so give them their chance...

25

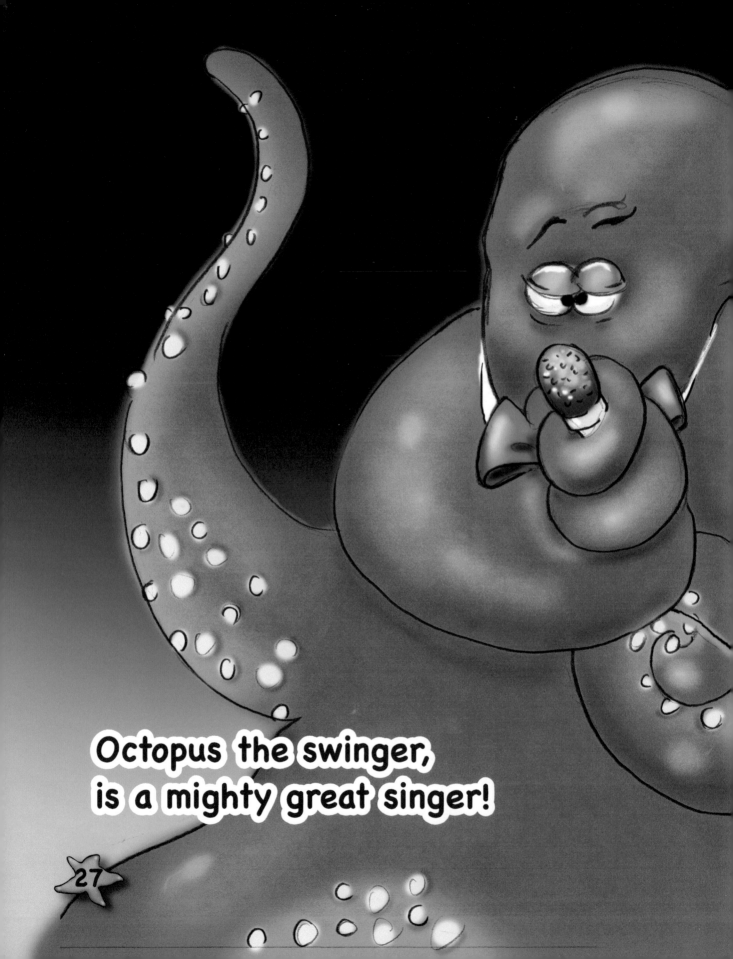

Octopus the swinger,
is a mighty great singer!

27

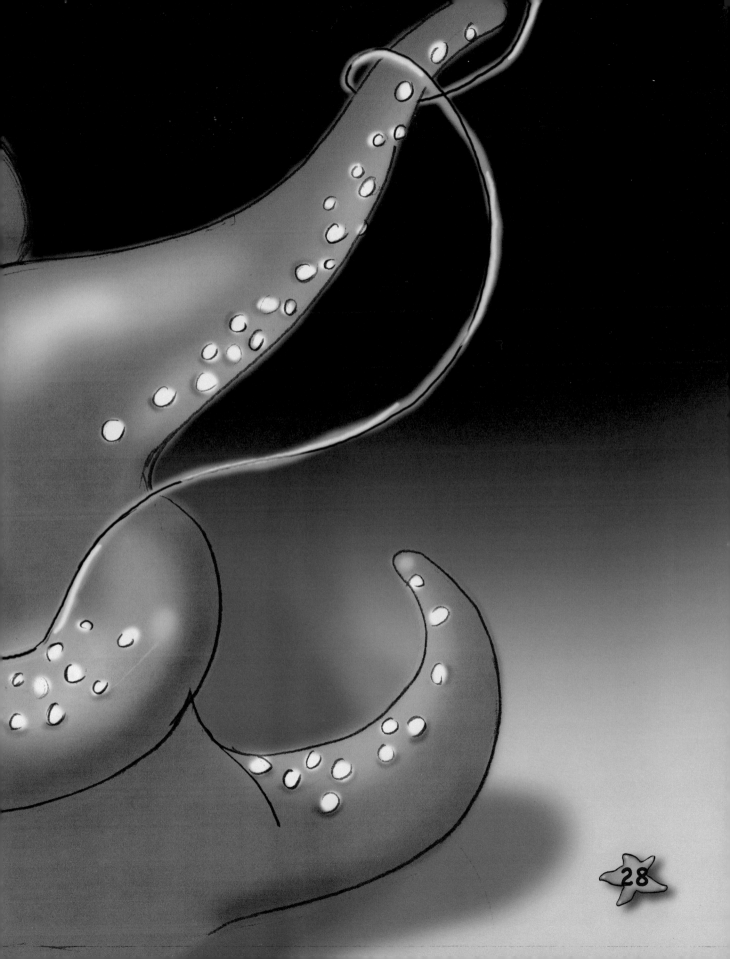

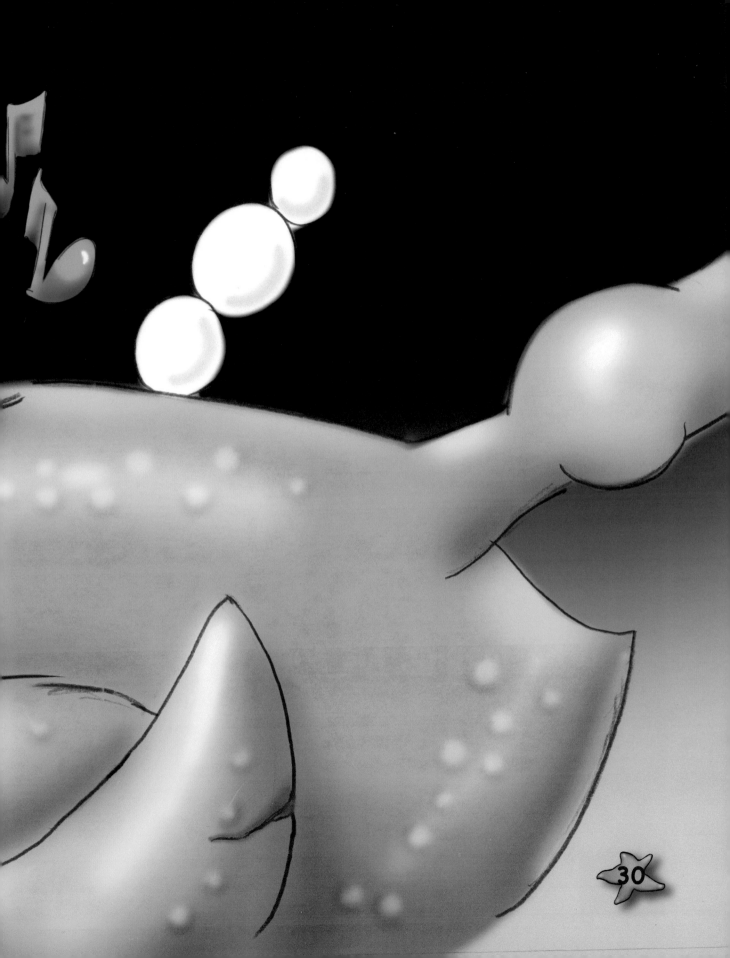

If Blue Lobster were here,
he'd be tapping his shoe.

31

33

So they danced and they partied.
It was a great night for all!
No one will forget
the Clam Digger's Ball!

34

Check out Robin's website for
new books and products!

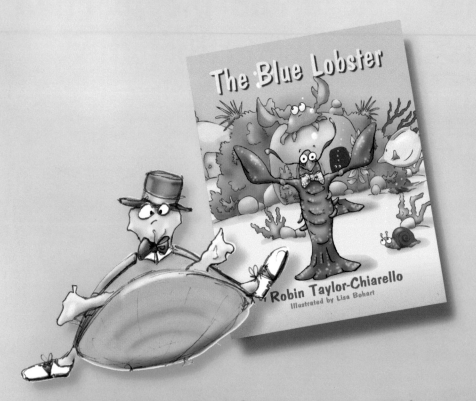

www.RobinTaylor-Chiarello.com

Watch for more adventures with
The Blue Lobster and his friends!

CPSIA information can be obtained
at www.ICGtesting.com
Printed in the USA
243748LV00001B